RAIN

For Amberly

A TEMPLAR BOOK

First published in the UK in 2016 by Templar Publishing,
part of the Bonnier Publishing Group,
The Plaza, 535 King's Road, London, SW10 0SZ
www.templarco.co.uk
www.bonnierpublishing.com

1 3 5 7 9 10 8 6 4 2

ISBN 978-1-78370-546-7 (Hardback)
ISBN 978-1-78370-547-4 (Paperback)

Designed by Genevieve Webster
Edited by Alison Ritchie

Printed in Lithuania

Sam Usher

RAIN

templar publishing

When I woke up this
morning, it was raining.

I couldn't wait to
get outside.

Grandad said perhaps it
was best to stay
indoors, but I said
I LIKE going out in
the rain.

You can do catching raindrops,

splashing in puddles,

and looking at everything
upside down.

But Grandad said,

"Let's wait for the rain to stop."

So we waited . . .

. . . and waited.

But did the rain stop?

So I said, "Grandad, I'd like to go on
a voyage with sea monsters."

And Grandad said, "Let's just wait
for the rain to stop."

But did the rain stop?

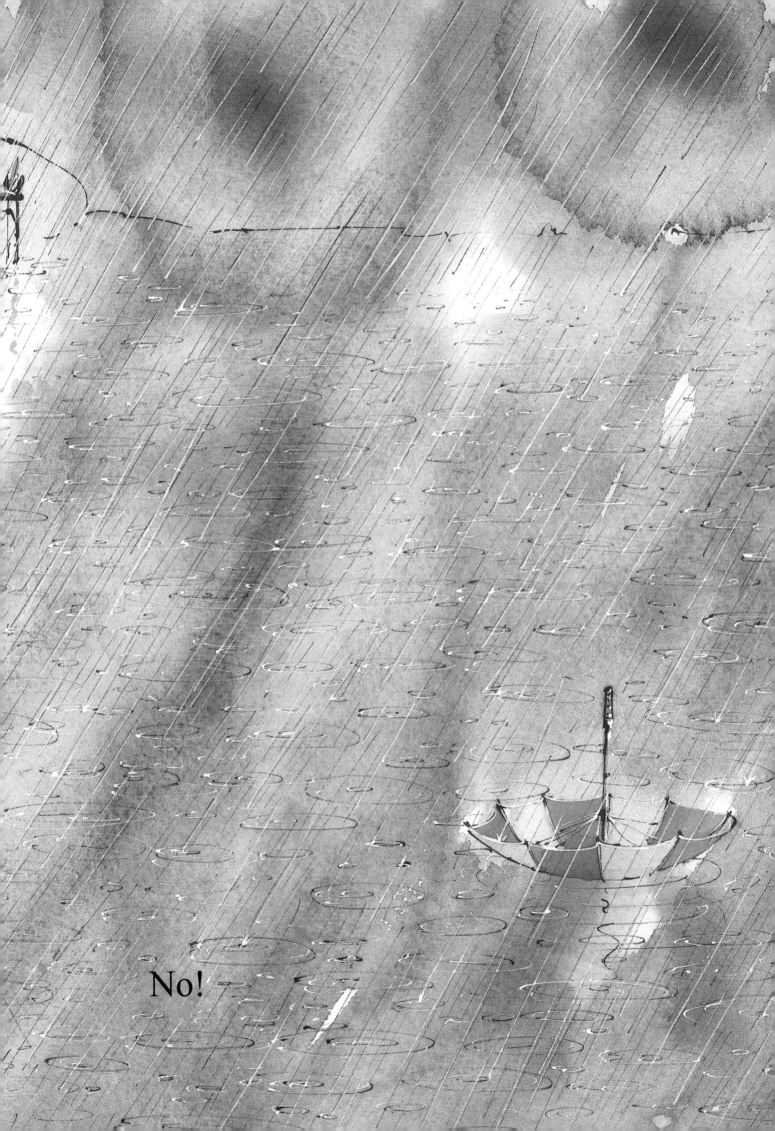

No!

So we waited some more.

And Grandad got on
with his writing.

I said, "Grandad,
I'd like to visit the floating city . . .

. . . with fancy dress acrobats
and carnivals and musical boatmen!"

And Grandad said . . .

"Quick! Let's go – we have
to catch the post!"

But had the rain stopped?

YES!

There wasn't a moment to lose.

So we made our preparations

and stepped outside.

It was time for a voyage at last.

Grandad made me captain.

It started to rain again . . .

. . . so we did catching raindrops.

And Grandad let me post his important letter.

Back on dry land,
with warm socks
and hot chocolate,
Grandad said,
"You see, the
very best things
are always worth
waiting for."

And I agreed.

I hope it rains
again tomorrow.